my itty-bitty bio

Stephen Curry

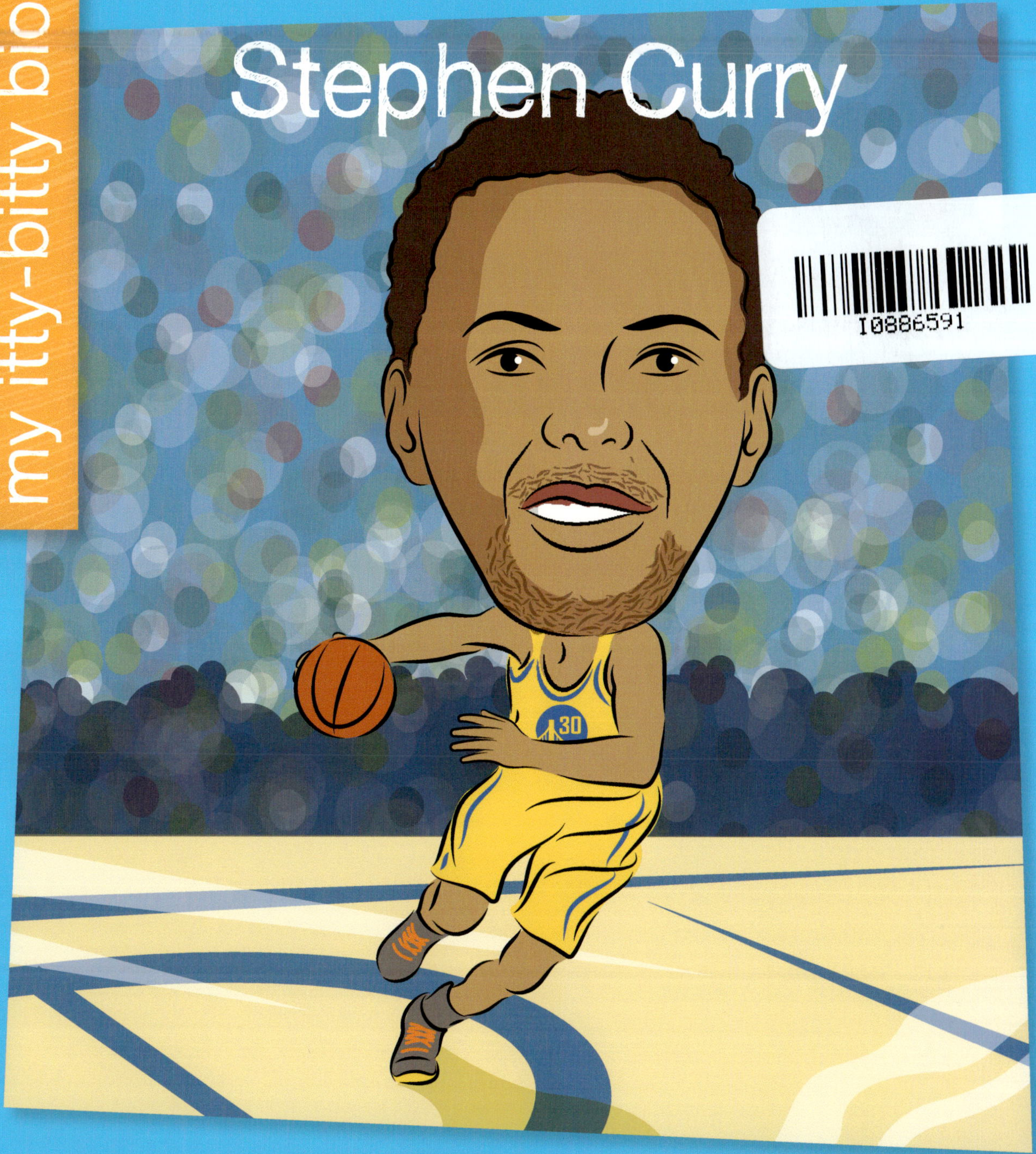

CHERRY LAKE PRESS

Published in the United States of America by Cherry Lake Publishing
Ann Arbor, Michigan
www.cherrylakepublishing.com

Reading Adviser: Marla Conn, MS, Ed., Literacy specialist, Read-Ability, Inc.
Book Designer: Jennifer Wahl
Illustrator: Jeff Bane

Photo Credits: ©Dmitrijs Kaminskis/Shutterstock, 5; ©Jerry Coli/Dreamstime, 7; ©Eric Broder Van Dyke/Dreamstime, 9, 22; ©Kevin Burkett/flickr, 11, 23; ©Kathy Hutchins/Shutterstock, 13; ©Philadelphia 76ers/flickr, 15; Courtesy of Nothing But Nets/Photo by Stuart Ramson, 17, 21; ©wavebreakmedia/Shutterstock, 19; Jeff Bane, cover, 1, 6, 10, 16

Library of Congress Cataloging-in-Publication Data

Names: Sarantou, Katlin, author. | Bane, Jeff, 1957- illustrator.
Title: Stephen Curry / Katlin Sarantou, Jeff Bane.
Description: Ann Arbor, Michigan : Cherry Lake Publishing, 2020. | Series: My itty-bitty bios | Includes index. | Audience: Grades K-1 | Summary: "The My Itty-Bitty Bio series are biographies for the earliest readers. This book examines the life of Stephen Curry in a simple, age-appropriate way that will help children develop word recognition and reading skills. Includes a table of contents, author biography, timeline, glossary, index, and other informative backmatter"-- Provided by publisher.
Identifiers: LCCN 2019034664 (print) | LCCN 2019034665 (ebook) | ISBN 9781534158801 (hardcover) | ISBN 9781534161108 (paperback) | ISBN 9781534159952 (pdf) | ISBN 9781534162259 (ebook)
Subjects: LCSH: Curry, Stephen 1988---Juvenile literature. | Basketball players--United States--Biography--Juvenile literature.
Classification: LCC GV884.C88 S27 2020 (print) | LCC GV884.C88 (ebook) | DDC 796.323092 [B]--dc23
LC record available at https://lccn.loc.gov/2019034664
LC ebook record available at https://lccn.loc.gov/2019034665

Printed in the United States of America
Corporate Graphics

table of contents

About the author: Katlin Sarantou grew up in the cornfields of Ohio. She enjoys reading and dreaming of faraway places.

About the illustrator: Jeff Bane and his two business partners own a studio along the American River in Folsom, California, home of the 1849 Gold Rush. When Jeff's not sketching or illustrating for clients, he's either swimming or kayaking in the river to relax.

my story

My name is Wardell Stephen Curry II. But most people call me Steph.

I was born on March 14, 1988.

Lorain
Cleveland
Parma
Akron

My dad played in the **NBA**.

I grew up loving and playing basketball.

What do you love to do?

I was **drafted** by the Golden State Warriors.

That's a team in California. I set records.

WARRIORS
State Farm
SPALDING

I was voted **Most Valuable Player** (MVP) twice. All 131 votes for MVP in 2016 were for me. That had never happened before.

CURRY
30

I **inspire** kids to work hard.

How do you inspire others?

I changed the game of basketball. I became famous for making **three-pointers**. Now more teams try to shoot them.

30
GEICO

I give to many **charities**. One is called Nothing But Nets. It fights **malaria** in Africa.

Nothing

I support girls in sports. I hosted a girls-only basketball camp. It was called It's Our Game.

I am a team player on and off the court. I use my fame to give back to others.

What would you like to ask me?

timeline

2009

1980

Born
1988

2016

2080

glossary & index

glossary

charities (CHAR-ih-teez) groups that raise money to help people in need

drafted (DRAFT-id) to be chosen by a sports team

inspire (in-SPIRE) to fill someone with a feeling or idea

malaria (muh-LAIR-ee-uh) a disease that people get from some mosquito bites

Most Valuable Player (MOHST VAL-yoo-buhl PLAY-ur) an award given to the best-performing player in a league

NBA (EN BEE AY) stands for the National Basketball Association, which is made up of many teams

three-pointers (three-POINT-urz) when the ball is thrown into the basket from a certain distance, scoring 3 points

index